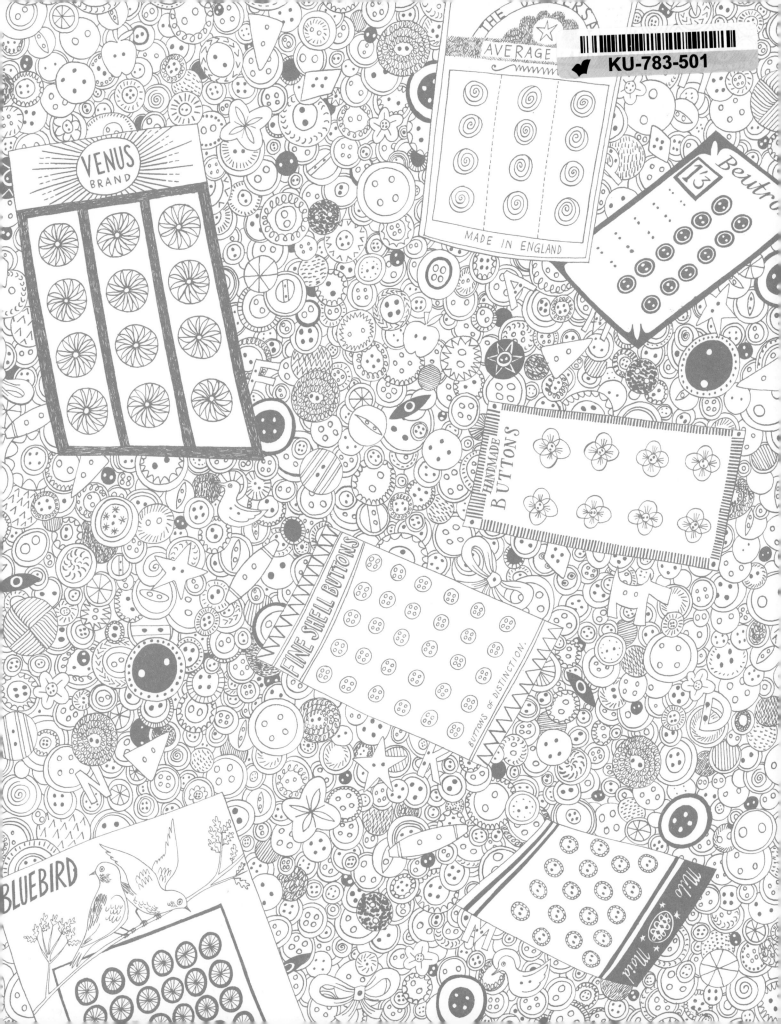

Paris Chic

HAMLYNS HATS

FOR MARK
love Em

For Felix
With love, Amy

First published by V&A Publishing, 2011
Victoria and Albert Museum
South Kensington
London SW7 2RL
www.vandapublishing.com

Hardback Edition
ISBN 978 1 85177 658 0

Paperback Edition
ISBN 978 1 85177 712 9

Designer: Emily Wilkinson
Editor: Susan Behar

Colour reproduction by Dot Gradations Ltd
Printed in China

HB
6 8 10 9 7 5
2017 2016

PB
4 6 8 10 9 7 5 3
2017 2016 2015 2014

A catalogue record for this book
is available from the British Library.

PANACHE
MILLINERS

RANDOLPHS

V&A Publishing
Supporting the world's leading
museum of art and design,
the Victoria and Albert
Museum, London

CLARA BUTTON
AND THE
MAGICAL
HAT DAY

written by AMY DE LA HAYE

illustrated by EMILY SUTTON

V&A Publishing

Clara Button sat on the living room floor,
choosing buttons to sew on to the hats and clothes
she made for her dolls and toy animals.

Suddenly her big brother, Ollie,
burst into the room on his skateboard
and the buttons went flying…

'Look what you've done!' yelled Clara.

'Who cares?' said Ollie. 'Buttons are sooo boring.'

He grabbed an old hat covered with daisies and
pulled it on top of his baseball cap. He made a silly face.

'That's Granny Elsie's hat,' cried Clara. 'Be careful.'

But it was too late.

Mum ran into the room.
'Oliver, you've torn Granny
Elsie's hat. What a very naughty
thing to do,' she scolded.

Granny Elsie had died
long before Clara and Ollie
were born. She had been
a milliner, which is someone
who makes beautiful hats.

Clara knew she would have loved
Granny Elsie because she liked making
hats too. Until now she had always worn
her granny's hat when she made them.
But now the special hat was broken.

The next day, to cheer Clara up, her mum asked if she would like to choose a special day out. Perhaps Clara might like to go swimming or to the cinema?
But Clara had other ideas. 'I would like a magical hat day please,' she said. Mum was not expecting this and so racked her brains as to where they might go.

Eventually she said, 'I know… we'll go to the Victoria and Albert Museum. It's full of wonderful things, including lots of hats.' Clara clapped her hands in delight.
'That'll be sooo boring,' grumbled Ollie.

Before they left the house
Clara tucked Granny Elsie's
hat into her backpack.
'If the museum is full of hats',
she thought, 'maybe I'll
find a milliner there
who can mend it.'

LIBERTY

SELFRIDGES

FORTNUM & MASON

HARVEY NICHOLS

HARRODS

On the bus to the museum,
Mum pointed out famous shops,
Ollie pretended to sleep
and Clara could only see hats – everywhere!

Clara thought the museum looked
like a palace. It was full of amazing
and beautiful things. She saw
imposing statues, glittering jewels,
silver and gold goblets and, above
her head, the strangest, sparkliest
sculpture. It had a label that read
'C H A N D E L I E R'.

Ollie yawned. He acted as if he was having a REALLY boring day. He even pretended not to see the tiger attacking a wooden soldier and the sharp, curving swords that brave warriors would have used in battle.

At last Mum, Ollie and Clara arrived in the Fashion Gallery. Clara looked around at all the gorgeous clothes in their large glass cases. She imagined herself as a model strutting down the catwalk, a princess dancing at a ball and an elegant lady wearing a gown covered in golden jewels.

Ollie yawned again. 'Okay Ollie,' said Mum, 'now let's
find something you'll like. Come along Clara.'
But Clara didn't hear her. All she could see was a beautiful
hat decorated with dancing shoes. It was being pulled along
on a trolley and she decided to follow it. Maybe it would
lead her to a milliner.

Clara followed the trolley through
a door into another room and found
herself in a huge cupboard brimming
with hats! Some looked like baskets, others
like bunches of flowers or presents tied up with
ribbon. One had a green bird perched on top
of it with beady eyes that stared straight at Clara.

'Grown-ups used to wear some
REALLY strange hats…' thought Clara.

'Hello' said a voice.

Clara turned around and saw a lady with long, curly red hair.

'Hello. My name is Clara,' said Clara, 'and I am looking
for a milliner.'

'A milliner?' asked the lady, surprised.

'Yes' said Clara.

The lady smiled and said, 'My name is Miranda and
I think we should find your parents. I'll call the security staff.'

While they waited, Miranda explained to Clara that she
was a Fashion Curator and that she looked after the many
hats in the museum's collections. Very carefully, as if picking
up a sleeping kitten, she took down a hat that looked like a
rock covered with sea creatures. Clara laughed. 'Granny Elsie
wouldn't have worn a hat like that!' she said.

The door opened and a man walked in.
'Are you a milliner?' asked Clara.
'Not exactly,' the man said, 'I'm
Edmund. I'm a sort of hat doctor.
Who are you?'
Clara introduced herself, then took
Granny Elsie's hat out of her bag.
'Look what my brother did!
He ruined Granny Elsie's hat,'
she said. The hat doctor
looked at Clara and
then at the hat.

He smiled.

'I can make it better.

And you can help me,' he said.

The next time the door opened
it was Clara's mum, Ollie, and
a man wearing a blue uniform.
Clara sighed loudly.
Her adventure was over.
'Clara!' said Mum. 'What
have you been up to?
And why is Granny's hat here?'
'We are mending it,' said Clara.
And she handed the hat doctor
a piece of thread.

Soon the hat was mended. Mum smiled and thanked Miranda,
Edmund and the security man at least seven times for being
so kind. 'Now what do you say, Clara?' she asked.

'Goodbye,' said Clara, 'and thank you.'
  Mum led Ollie and Clara to the museum's cafe
    where they drank hot chocolate and ate delicious cake.

That night, Clara dreamt she was
flying through a galaxy of hats
– a 'millinerium' –

as she lay on the brim
of Granny Elsie's newly mended hat.

Meanwhile, in the next room,
Ollie was having very different dreams...

·BLOWN GLASS CHANDELIER·

·BY ARTIST DALE CHIHULY 1992·

·TIPU'S TIGER ~ A MECHANICAL ORGAN·

·MADE IN INDIA IN 1793·

·VERY HIGH HEELED SHOES WITH PLATFORMS·

·BY DESIGNER VIVIENNE WESTWOOD 1993·

·HAT FOR EATING BOUILLABAISSE (FISH STEW)·

·BY ARTIST EILEEN AGAR 1937·

· 'PAS DE DEUX' ~ A HAT WITH BALLET SHOES ·

· BY MILLINER STEPHEN JONES 1982 ·

· AN EMBROIDERED SILK DRESS CALLED A MANTUA ·

· MADE OVER 200 YEARS AGO TO BE WORN AT A PALACE ·

· STEEL HUNTING SWORD WITH IVORY GRIP ·

· MADE IN ENGLAND IN THE 1650s ·

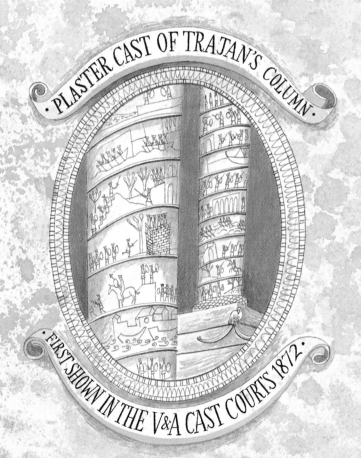

· PLASTER CAST OF TRAJAN'S COLUMN ·

· FIRST SHOWN IN THE V&A CAST COURTS 1872 ·